Lost and Found in JumpStart Town

by Joan Holub

Illustrated by Duendes Del Sur

SCHOLASTIC INC.

New York Toronto London Auckland Sydney
Mexico City New Delhi Hong Kong

The JumpStart gang
all shout, "Hooray!
Let's go to JumpStart
Town today."

When they get to town
they dash everywhere.
There go Eleanor, Kisha,
Casey, and Pierre!

The four friends forget
sticking together is smart.
They run different ways,
each one off with a start.

The bakery has cakes
all in a row.
Eleanor's box
has a pretty **blue** bow.

"Where are my friends?
I wish I knew."

Uh-oh. Eleanor is lost!
What will she do?

In the toy store in town
is a doll dressed in **green**.

It's the prettiest doll
Kisha has ever seen.

"Where are my friends?
I wish I knew."
Uh-oh. Kisha is lost!
What will she do?

Casey sees workers
with bright **yellow** hats.
They are building apartments
for families of cats.

"Where are my friends?
I wish I knew."

Uh-oh. Casey is lost!
What will he do?

Pierre sees firefighters
with a **red** water hose.
Whoosh! Splish! Splash!
Out the fire goes!

"Where are my friends?
I wish I knew."
Uh-oh. Pierre is lost!
What will he do?

Zoom, vroom, zoom!
What is that sound?

Kisha, Casey, and Pierre
look up, down, and around.

Then the three lost friends
look wa-a-a-ay up high.
Wow! Look who is flying
a plane in the sky!

They run to the park —
one, two, three, four!

The JumpStart gang
is not lost anymore.

Munch, munch, munch!
Crunch, crunch, crunch!
The JumpStart gang
is ready for lunch.

Then Casey runs off
to the jungle gym.

"Wait!" call his friends
as they try to stop him.

Friends should stick together
in whatever they do.
So they'll never get lost . . .

. . . and neither will you!